I0639845

Thomas Applegate

The Precious Gift

Thomas Applegate

The Precious Gift

ISBN/EAN: 9783337780401

Printed in Europe, USA, Canada, Australia, Japan

Cover: Foto ©Andreas Hilbeck / pixelio.de

More available books at **www.hansebooks.com**

THE

PRECIOUS GIFT.

BY THE LATE
REV. THOMAS APPLEGATE,

AUTHOR OF

"THE VOICE OF SACRED TRIPLES," "THE FRUITS OF THE SPIRIT,"
"SACRED GEOGRAPHY AND HISTORY," ETC.

FIRST THOUSAND.

GENEVA, N. Y
L. W. APPLEGATE,
1872.

PREFACE

—

FEW words are necessary in laying before the public the second volume of the works of the late Rev. Thomas Applegate.

The warm reception, with which " The Voice of Sacred Triples" has been received; and the earnest request of many for another such work, has induced us to place in the hands of devout readers, a volume which, we feel confident to affirm, will be perused with equal profit and pleasure.

Its pages are designed to explain the preciousness of that gift which we received from our heavenly FATHER, in the person of HIS SON JESUS CHRIST.

With the sincere hope that this work may be a companion for the Christian in-the hours of meditation and devotion; and be the means to aid him in his heavenward journey, we humbly submit its pages to the earnest attention of the reader.

A.

'CONTENTS.

THE PRECIOUS GIFT.

CHAPTER I.

THE DESIRE OF ALL NATIONS.

THE evidence of prophecy is the most satisfactory and convincing—the most direct, interesting and impressive, from its germinant and growing character, by which it ripens into history, and is brought out from the keeping of the past, and placed within the limits of each one's personal study, observation and experience. If it had no other feature than this, it would be amply sufficient to impart to it all the charm of personal discovery, and to produce in the mind a thrill of unspeakable delight. The student who grasps it finds that he is holding in his hand the last link of a chain that has come down to him from the earliest ages, and is passing on to the men of that generation who will witness the last act of this

world's drama, when the angel shall swear by
Him that liveth for ever and ever that time shall
be no longer. There is, indeed, in prophecy, such
an accumulation of proof upon proof—such a
chain of evidence for thousands of years, and such
growing strength in the attestations from one
period to another, that when the subject is fairly
investigated the conclusion is irresistible—"This
is the finger of God." The predictions that announce the coming of the Messiah belong to the
most interesting of the group ; and as we contem-
plate them in the beauty and precision of their
accomplishment, they lead to the happiest effect.

The ancients inform us that when Orpheus
played upon his harp, the wild beasts thronged
around him as listening spectators. If this were
literally correct we should suppose that the beasts
of the forest were only affected by the music while
they heard it, and that it did not actually change
their natures and make lions as lambs. The
music of ancient prediction has sometimes op-
erated on the minds of men in a similar way.
There were many who heard with emotion the
discourses of the Saviour, but their goodness
was as the morning cloud, and the early dew that

passeth away. And so among the numbers that listened to the sublime declarations of the prophets, there were not a few who gave the fondest hopes of piety and usefulness, while their subsequent history proved too plainly that they had returned again to their obduracy and unbelief. Still there were some, as there always have been, disposed to speak of the glory of CHRIST's Kingdom, and to talk of His power. The pious Jews, in the time of Haggai, were anxious to rebuild the temple, and have the worship of GOD speedily restored. But when the foundations were laid they met with discouragement from others, who, remembering the magnificence of the former temple, wept on thinking how far the second would fall short of it. The prophet sought to allay their grief by assuring them that, inferior as the second temple might appear in comparison to Solomon's, yet the glory of this latter house should be greater than that of the former. He assigned as a reason that it should be graced with the presence and teachings of CHRIST. "The LORD whom ye seek shall suddenly come to His temple: even the Messenger of the Covenant whom ye delight in; behold He shall come, saith the

LORD of hosts." The time of His advent is thus
indicated as close at hand. The Saviour was to
make His appearance in the second temple. The
signs of the times told them that they were standing on the very threshold of the event. The waiting Church had already passed over five epochs of
its journey—the distance from Adam to Noah—
from Noah to Abraham—from Abraham to Moses
—from Moses to the temple of Solomon—thence
to the captivity; and now only one stage more
remained, the sixth day's journey, and the Shiloh
would come.

The epithet applied to the Saviour is as beautiful as it is expressive—the Desire of all nations.
This was so literally correct that the men of every
country seemed to be looking out for Him as a
benefactor. Everywhere, near and remote, among
the civilized and the rude, the people were strong-
ly impressed with a belief that a deliverer was
about to appear. Among the testimonies of heathen writers is a little poem of Virgil's, written a
few years only before the birth of CHRIST, and
which contains a prophecy that some extraordinary personage would shortly come, and restore
peace and plenty, and the manifold blessings of

the golden reign. The writer may have been indebted, in some degree, to ancient tradition, partly founded on the promises of GOD respecting the seed of the woman, traces of which through much corruption, had not worn out; and partly to the dispersion of the children of Israel, whose imperfect accounts of Scripture, mixed up with much that was fabulous, would contribute to keep alive the expectation of the desired event. The sentiment was certainly derived originally from a divine source—the early and oft-repeated promise of the Messiah that was to come.

The prophets, who predicted Him, were so thoroughly persuaded of the truth of what they wrote, that they were not afraid to risk their reputation and standing with their nation upon the far off issues. Fifteen hundred years before CHRIST, Moses pledged himself that a prophet-like unto himself should arise in Judea; and he esteemed the reproach of CHRIST greater riches than the treasures of Egypt. At a period still earlier, the patriarch Job declared that the Redeemer lived and would appear on the earth. He believed in Him as One who would justify and eternally save him. Abraham rejoiced to see His day, and he saw it, and was glad. Balaam, in the land of Moab, was favored in his blindness with dim glimpses of the truth. He saw the vision of the Almighty. He fell into a trance, but his eyes were open. When a neighboring prince sought him for his divination against the power of Israel he said, "How shall I curse whom the LORD hath not cursed? or how shall I defy whom the LORD hath not defied?" He then burst forth into the noblest strain of poetry, and painted, in words that burn, the fortunes of the chosen people, "How goodly are thy tents, O Jacob, and thy tabernacles, O Israel. As the valleys are they spread forth; as gardens by the river's side; as the trees of lign-aloes, which the LORD hath planted, and as cedar trees beside the waters." The wrath of Balak was aroused. He threatened where he could not buy. But the menace and the bribe were both in vain. "If Balak would give me his house full of silver and gold," said he, "I cannot go beyond the commandment of the Lord, to do either good or bad, of mine own mind; but what the LORD saith, that will I speak." Then with the composure of one who casts himself on GOD, he uttered, as the LORD had taught him, his wondrous prophecy of CHRIST, "I shall see Him, but not now: I shall behold Him, but not nigh: there shall come a Star out of Jacob, and a Sceptre shall rise out of Israel." This prophecy was given two hundred and fifty years before the Trojan war—six hundred years before Homer—seven centuries before the founding of the Roman Empire by Romulus; and twelve centuries before Alexander the Great. So true is it that one day is with the LORD as a thousand years, and a thousand years as one day. In the meantime David gloried in identifying all his credit, both as a king and a poet, with his predictions of the sufferings and triumphs of CHRIST. The sublime Isaiah hazarded all the glory of his immortal genius and royal descent in foretelling the little incidents of the nativity. The prophet Daniel staked his character and reputation upon the exact time of CHRIST's coming. And the prophet Micah, with equal candor, announced the place of His birth. Some of these prophecies were so minute that they mention the very tone of voice in which the Saviour would conduct His ministry on earth; and the particular kind and age of the animal on which He would ride triumphantly into Jerusalem "upon a colt, the foal of an ass." All this is the more remarkable because they understood not fully, at the time, the things they were writing. St. Peter says, " All of them searched diligently to discover what or what manner of time, the Spirit of CHRIST which was in them did signify, when it testified beforehand the sufferings of CHRIST, and the glory that should follow." They knew that GOD had spoken the subject of their communications; and they were willing to stand or fall in public estimation upon the result of what they stated, touching this long-promised— long-looked for, and much desired King.

The coming of CHRIST was the desire of all nations because He had the disposal of the very blessings which all nations need. Do nations need light? He is the light of the world. The object of His mission was to bless all the nations of the earth, by turning them from darkness to light, and from the worship of dumb idols to serve the living and true GOD. If we could suppose a nation enveloped for ages in Egyptian darkness—darkness that may be felt, though the people had no just conception of light, yet it might be said to be their desire, inasmuch as it would improve their condition. There were some among the heathen who were willing to acknowledge that they were wandering in dubious paths, bewildered and perplexed—thirsting for light and information, and knew not how to obtain it. They had fears and forebodings, and felt their guilt and weakness, but knew not of a remedy. Under the troubles of life they had no supernatural support; and in adversity and death they would offer "thousands of rams, and rivers of oil, and give the first born for their transgression, the fruit of their body for the sin of their soul." Do nations need strength? The name of the LORD is a strong tower, into which the righteous run and are safe. He is a stronghold for the prisoners of hope. All power belongs to Him in heaven and in earth. Do nations need riches? His riches are unsearchable —durable riches and righteousness. Do nations need friends? He is a friend that sticketh closer than a brother. Do nations applaud benevolence? His love passeth knowledge. "He delivers the needy when he crieth, the poor also, and him that hath no helper." He comprises in Himself all that the exigencies of man can require, in every country and clime, and is the Desire of all natious, just as a physician, able and willing to cure all diseases, is the desire of all patients.

The coming of CHRIST was attended with signs and wonders. The holy purpose was fulfilled, "I will shake the heavens and the earth, and the sea, and the dry land. I will shake all nations." The scene was one of stupendous magnificence and grandeur that ranged through all the powers of creation, and was fraught with overwhelming results to our future destiny. As no trivial matter could have induced the SON of the HIGHEST to have undertaken such an embassy, it seemed befitting that the magnitude of His mission should be marked with phenomena of more than ordinary occurrence. When the law was given on Sinai, the mountain shook to its base. Thunderings and lightnings, and thick darkness filled the air. The people trembled at the sight, and Moses said, "I exceedingly fear and quake." When Israel came out of Egypt, a passage was made through the sea by the waters dividing, and the LORD caused the sea to go back by a strong east wind all that night, and made the sea dry land. When the migratory host were in the wilderness, streams were brought out of the rock by the rod of Moses; manna was rained down from heaven by a constant miracle, and a cloudy, fiery pillar directed their journeys. So when the Day-spring from on High visited us, the shadows of the Jewish Dispensation fled—the apparatus of the old economy was superceded—the forms of heathen worship shrunk from their accustomed grandeur —the priests grew pale—the fires upon the altars flickered—the very gods upon Olympus shivered and were dismayed. The little town of Bethlehem became flushed with life and excitement— the scene of stir and animation. The Inn was crowded with tax-payers, drawn from the adjacent country by the edict of Augustus Cæsar; and the infant JESUS made His appearance in a stable, wrapped in swaddling clothes and laid in a manger. The midnight sky is radiant with more than earthly light. The music of celestial songs falls upon the ear. There is a fluttering of angels' wings, and the air is fragrant with angels' breath. The wise men upon the Persian hills are watching the stars. They are looking out for Balaam's star to rise. They scan with keenest search the radiant maze. They have made sure of every speck of light, though ever so small. They have measured every space of blue, however scant. Now, there gleams on their vision a stranger orb. A new light kindles in the heavens. The star of Bethlehem shines. It travels westward towards Judea. Its brilliancy gives presage to some new and glorious dynasty. The Magi rise in haste and prepare for their journey. They store themselves with royal gifts of purest gold. They fill their censers with the finest flakes of Arabian frankincense. They provide as a part of their freight a suitable quantity of Abyssinian myrrh. They start upon their search, and the star precedes them to Jerusalem. They ask in that Metropolis, "Where is He that is born king of the Jews? for we have seen His star in the east, and are come to worship Him." The great mass of the people were unable to answer the question, but the chief priests and scribes informed them, from the sacred roll, "In Bethlehem of Judea." The star that disappeared during their continuance in the city, now resumed its place—conducted the visitors to Bethlehem, and dropped so low as to signalize the house where the young child was. The star pointed out the Star. The starry orb showed "the Root and Offspring of David, the bright and morning Star."

"Sceptre and Star Divine, Who in Thy inmost shrine
Hast made us worshippers, O claim Thine own.
More than Thy seers we know—
O teach our love to grow up to Thy heavenly light."

The star dies out above that humble dwelling just as the Magi enter it; and opening their treasures, they present unto the Holy JESUS gifts, gold, frankincense and myrrh. It was the custom of the country to show external honor to illustrious personages; and this they manifested by the richest offerings it was in their power to make. They were loyal men, whose devout affections were deep enough, and whose love and joy, and gratitude were intense enough to prompt this royal, tangible, and substantial offering of their sincere devotion.

CHRIST came to reign king in Zion, and the establishment of His kingdom demanded the complete overthrow of whatever was opposed to it. The Jews had been the most favored people under heaven, to whom pertained the adoption, and the glory, and the covenants, and the giving of the law, and the service of GOD, and the promises. But they rejected CHRIST, and filled up the measure of their iniquity by putting Him to death. Often would He have gathered them together as a hen gathereth her chickens under her wings, but they

would not.   They preferred to be naked and destitute, rather than to be covered with His feathers.
Their house was therefore to be left unto them
destitute.   The Romans destroyed their city and
temple, and made it a capital crime for a Jew to
set his foot in Jerusalem.   Their banishment from
Judea was only the prelude to their expulsion from
city to city, and from kingdom to kingdom, until
in the wide world they could find no rest for the
soles of their feet.   But of all surprising phenomena
there is perhaps none so wonderful as their main-
taining through so many long centuries their distinguished features.   That they should be dispersed
into all nations, and yet amalgamate with none;
that they should be everywhere found, and yet be
everywhere the same;   that they should submit
themselves to all forms of government, and adopt
all varieties of customs, and yet retain all their
national characteristics is inexplicable, except as
the fulfilment of prophecy.   The separate condition of the Jews is a living miracle of the truth—
a standing memento of their guilt in rejecting
the promised Saviour.   Nor is the continued infidelity of the Jews a jot less remarkable.   Whatever probability there was that they would reject

Christianity on its first publication, it was a probability that diminished with every miracle that was wrought; and every rolling year, as it brought no other Messiah, only swelled the demonstration that JESUS was the CHRIST. Their own prophecies had clearly determined that CHRIST would come while the second temple was standing and at the close of the seventy weeks from the termination of the Babylonish captivity. But when the second temple was demolished, and the seventy weeks, on every possible computation, had long ago expired, we should have supposed that they would have been compelled to admit either that CHRIST was the long promised Messiah, or that their expectation was vain. There seemed no alternative if they rejected JESUS of Nazareth, but the rejection of their own scriptures.

Never therefore should we meet a Jew, without feeling that we meet the strongest witness for the truth of our holy religion. The exile of the race, for their iniquity, agreeably to the declarations of our LORD, eighteen hundred years ago, and their continued disappointment of a deliverer, is one of the noblest proofs that, the desire of all nations has come, and that they need not look for another.

CHAPTER II.

THE FULNESS OF TIME.

———

FOUR thousand years rolled away between the
bestowment of the promise to our first parents in
Eden that the seed of the woman should bruise
the serpent's head, and its actual fulfilment. And
if we ask the question, Why was CHRIST born into
the world at so late a date? Why was not Christianity introduced at once? the most appropriate
answer is, CHRIST came thus late that scoffers
might find no excuse for their unbelief. The
blessing was delayed so long because the world
was not fitted by its population and its general
state, to receive it earlier. There was as much
propriety in this delay, as there is in not allowing
a minor to come into the full possession of the
property to which he is an heir. "The heir,"
said the Apostle, "differeth nothing from a servant as long as he is a child, though he be Lord
of all, but is under tutors and governors until the
time appointed of the Father." "Even so we,

when we were children, were in bondage under the elements of the world." "But when the fulness of time was come, GOD sent forth His SON, made of a woman, made under the law to redeem them that were under the law, that we might receive the adoption of sons." The intimation here given is, that it would be as unwise for GOD to have sent His SON into the world at an earlier period, as it would be to allow a minor to become the master of his property before he becomes of age.

It is not always easy to discover the reasons that actuate the Divine mind, though we may be fully assured they are such as to justify the course He adopts in the administration of His affairs. Could we see, as He does, the end from the beginning, we should acknowledge readily the rectitude of His procedure, and exclaim, "Just and true are thy ways, Thou king of saints."

If CHRIST had come during the antediluvian age, or at the time of the flood, the donation of such an unspeakable gift, at that period of the world's history, would have been most unsuitable. It does not appear that there was any one then living capable of presenting the account of it in such a

manner as to interest the people of all subsequent
times. Whoever had taken upon himself the
office of historiographer would not probably have
been very successful in benefitting mankind at
large. Had he written to suit us, upon whom
the ends of the world are come, the general style
of the composition would have been ill adapted
to his own contemporaries. And had he written
so as to suit them, the narrative would have been
of little practical service to us. But the Saviour,
by not appearing in the world till civilization and
letters had become more common, afforded every
facility to men to herald and announce His mission; to examine His claims, and to discover how
the Old Testament writings are fulfilled in those
of the New.

If the Saviour had made His appearance in
the interim, between the Flood and the time of
Moses, the population of the globe was then com-
paratively small. There would have been but few
to see Him, and but very few to appreciate Him.
And when we consider the sublime doctrines
which He taught, the salutary precepts which He
delivered, the miracles which He performed, and
His spotless life, we say, and say justly, there was

wisdom in the plan of withholding the bestowment of such a blessing from the few, when it
was intended to meet the wants of our race in
every region of the globe.

The time from Moses to the Prophets would
have been too soon. The people were not then
prepared for the event. The Jews were not suffi-
ciently informed of the grounds of salvation.
They had but just emerged from Egypt, with all
the associations of idolatry fresh in their minds.
It was, therefore, befitting the dignity and grandeur of the Messiah, that His coming should be
deferred, and that the types and shadows should
still retain their significancy, to light up the
darkness of night, till the day-star should arise in
their hearts.

The period of the four great monarchies would
have been equally inappropriate. The thoughts
and passions of men were too much absorbed in
warfare, to gain for the religion of CHRIST any
thing like an ascendency over the public mind.
If it should have happened to triumph, persons
would not have been wanting to affirm that Christianity was the invention of the Nimrods and the
Nebuchadnezzars to maintain the views of des-

potic government and keep the people in subjection. But to place the matter beyond the power of the enemy, GOD purposely delayed the coming of His SON until the Augustan age, when the blessings of peace, civilization and philosophy were abundantly diffused. Nor were the people losers by the delay. Though they had not the same amount of light and information that subsequent generations enjoyed, yet they had the same unqualified promise, that whoever looked by faith to the LAMB of GOD, would assuredly be saved. They knew that the atonement which CHRIST would offer, would avail alike for the sins committed under the first covenant, and under the second—that penitents were all pardoned and renewed, and finally admitted into heaven upon trust or sufferance on the ground of faith in Him, who was to come in due time.

Due time and fulness of time are synonymous, and refer to the period when Cæsar Augustus lived. That was the fulness of time most emphatically; and the best adapted for introducing the Saviour and His Gospel. The minds of men were then more at rest, and better prepared to detect Him, if He had been an impostor. Both

Jews and Gentiles had political motives to urge them to the strictest vigilance. The Jews were under the Roman yoke, and looked to the Messiah as their deliverer. He was a bright star in their horizon, and they were disposed to scrutinize His character with the nicest accuracy. The heads of the Roman Government were also very jealous of losing any portion of their influence, and they would, consequently, investigate His authority with equal diligence. The two parties had been ably disciplined and matured for the task by the system of argumentation that had been introduced. The policy they pursued was to doubt and dispute every thing they met with, and to admit nothing without proof. Christianity, therefore, threw down the gauntlet, and challenged the closest research. The collisions and disputes that ensued only served to rub the diadem into brightness, and to manifest to all that CHRIST was the only begotten SON of GOD.

Men's minds, at the time of our LORD's Advent, were much perplexed in reference to the doctrine of immortality. The idea was almost expunged from the general creed. The practice of suicide had become exceedingly popular. Still, the love

of life in the majority was too ardent to allow of
its being readily given up. Just at that particular
juncture, when information was so much needed,
CHRIST came, and brought life and immortality
to light. He came, a light to enlighten the Gentiles, and the glory of His people Israel. The
darkness that brooded over the sepulchre He
instantly dissipated, and caused to shine into it
the bright beams of day. Standing upon the
portals of the tomb, and addressing Himself to
the promiscuous throng which the majesty and
loveliness of His person drew around Him, He
could exclaim, with an emphasis which belonged
to no earthly being, "I am the Resurrection and
the Life." "If a man keep My sayings, he shall
never see death." This was the boon for which
they had so ardently panted. This put them in
possession of a treasure that revealed the highest
source of enjoyment for the life that now is, and
for that which is to come. At no previous period
could these tidings have been promulgated so
successfully. There was no time but that which
St. Paul calls the fulness of time, when the state
of the nations afforded such numerous facilities.
Little did the Romans think, when they con-

structed their Appian ways, and opened up new roads, that they were forming paths for the Gospel to track its way over the then known world. Little did they suppose, when they reduced their language to rule, that they were multiplying the means of defrauding their own temples, and dethroning their own gods.

The Greek language was now generally spoken, and thus constituted an appropriate vehicle to embody and express the glorious gospel of the Blessed GOD. This would seem to be one reason why the time of CHRIST's coming was so long postponed. The advent was unquestionably delayed, that there might be prepared the means for transmitting the glad tidings of salvation in the most expressive and permanent shape. The language in which the New Testament truths were to be preached had now become the language of so many cultivated nations, that a truth spoken in Greek would find an echo everywhere, while the same truth uttered in Hebrew, would scarcely have been understood beyond the borders of Judea. It was therefore a special Providence in anticipation of the Advent, that one language, and that the noblest and the grandest, should very

much dominate and prevail. Hence, the word
of salvation went forth as the day breaks with
gradually increasing light, and where it poured
its meridian splendor, it eclipsed all other lights
in its surpassing brightness. It grew as the mus-
tard seed, which, when sown, is the least of all
seeds, and when grown is the greatest of all herbs.
It rose as the fountain rises, a spring of living
water, swelling into a river, "the streams whereof
make glad the city of GOD." Its voice is more
powerful than thunder; and its echo softer than
the summer breeze. It would seem as though
the universe was purposely constructed to repeat
its sound. It was whispered in the East, and
rolled round to the West. It was repeated in the
West and rolls back to the East. It is gentle and
fructifying as a spring shower. It is all-embrac-
ing, vivifying and enlightening as the sun. It is
all-glorious and eternal as the heaven to which it
leads.

There was another very remarkable feature
that characterized the fulness of time, and which
much facilitated the labors of the ambassadors of
CHRIST—the political consolidation of nations.
Two or three hundred years previously the nations

of the earth were in such a state of internal antagonism, that an inhabitant of one country could not
cross over the frontiers, and sojourn even for a
short time in another. But owing to the conquests of Alexander, and afterwards of the Cæsars, the whole civilized world became consolidated into one empire; and an appeal to Cæsar
was a sufficient protection in almost every capital
and village of the habitable globe. This was the
result of the movements and changes of four
thousand years; the stirring of the waters, prior
to the descent of the angel, to impregnate them
with the elements of permanent and universal
health. And when the world was thus prepared
for the Advent—when the people were at peace—
when a language had been formed fitted to convey
the truths of the Gospel—when the nations of the
earth had become consolidated and made accessible to the feet of them that bring glad tidings of
great joy; then CHRIST came—then the Sun of
Righteousness arose—then the beginning of the
Gospel of the SON of GOD was heard—the monop-
oly of a few became the privilege and the right
of all—the national cistern became a world-wide
fountain—the lamp of Jerusalem was exchanged

for the bright sun in the sky, for the benefit of the whole race.

The manner of the Incarnation added to our dignity and glory. GOD sent forth His SON, made of a woman. There is a peculiarity in the expression *made* of a woman, which does not agree with our ordinary mode of speaking. It is a truth that stands out by itself, applying only to CHRIST. More frequently it is said *born* of a woman. We understand, in either sense, that He took upon Himself our nature,. and became bone of our bone and` flesh of our flesh. "The Word was made flesh, and dwelt among us." "Because the children were partakers of flesh and blood, He also partook part of the same." It behoved Him in all things to be made like unto His brethren, that He might be a merciful and faithful High Priest in all things pertaining to GOD, to make reconciliation for the sins of the people. It was not that CHRIST was merely the brother of every man that constituted the excellency of the Incarnation. A man and his brother are walled off and separated by their personality. What is done by the one cannot properly be felt as the action of the other. But CHRIST by becoming human as well as divine took as it were a part of every man—tied Himself up, if we may so speak, by a most sensitive fibre to every member of the human family. Along those unnumbered threads of endearment and sympathy there came traveling the evil deeds and evil thoughts of an evil and rebellious seed. Loudly they knocked at His heart, and asked for vengeance, and thus the wondrous result was brought about, that He who did no sin, neither was guile found in His mouth, felt the sins that we have committed, was pierced and torn by them, and suffered, the just for the unjust, that He might bring us to GOD. To accomplish this mighty task, the Son of the Highest condescended to present Himself in our world as a feeble infant. This shows that the errand on which He came, was one of pure, disinterested benevolence and mercy, and that GOD sent not His SON into the world to condemn the world, but that the world through Him might be saved. He came not as a man of war arrayed in the attributes of terror, but as a helpless babe, in humble life, wrapped in swaddling clothes and lying in a manger. Had He been born in a palace, or dwelt among the rich and the great, the poor might have feared to approach Him. But by taking the lowest scale in society, the poorest and most dejected of men may have hope for acceptance. A description of the person of JESUS, as He appeared in the discharge of His ministry, is preserved in an ancient manuscript, that bears the name of Publius Latilus, President to the Senate of Rome; and it is remarkably interesting as showing a beautiful coincidence between the views of the writer, and the testimony of Holy Scripture. "There lives," says he, "at this time in Judea a man of singular character whose name is JESUS CHRIST. The Barbarians esteem Him as a prophet, and His followers adore Him as the immediate offspring of the immortal GOD. He is endowed with such unparalleled virtues as to call back the dead from their graves, and to heal every kind of disease with a word or a touch. His person is tall and elegantly shaped, His aspects amiable and reverent, His hair flows in those beauteous shades which no colors can match, falling in graceful curls below His ears, agreeably crouching upon His shoulders, and parting upon the crown of His head. His dress is of the sect of the Nazarites. His forehead is smooth and large. His cheek is without spot save that of a lovely

red. His nose and mouth are formed with exquisite symmetry. His beard is thick and suitable
to the hair of His head, reaching a little below
His chin, and parting in the middle like a fold.
His eyes are bright, clear, and serene. He re-
bukes with mildness and writes with the most
tender and persuasive language. His whole
address, whether in word or deed, is elegant,
grave, and strictly characteristic of so exalted a
being. No man has seen Him laugh, but the
whole world has seen Him weep frequently, and
so persuasive are his tears that the whole multitude cannot withhold their tears from joining
in sympathy with Him. He is very modest,
temperate, and wise. In short whatever this
phenomenon may turn out to be in the end, He
seems at present to be a man of excellent and
divine perfection, every way surpassing the children of men." Thus far we have a delineation of
the Saviour, both able, and beautiful, from a
heathen contemporary. We are thankful for the
portraiture, as corroborative of sacred history,
that represents Him in His lovliness, as the chief
among ten thousand and the one altogether lovely.

Notice we now the benefits of CHRIST's incarnation. They are two fold—redemption and adoption. These two cardinal blessings of our holy religion go hand in hand. Without the former, the latter could never be realized but as a thing of nought. Neither of them is intended to release us from the obligations of the law, but from the penalty which it denounces. And CHRIST hath redeemed us from the curse of the law, having been made a curse for us. CHRIST is the end of the law for righteousness to every one that believeth. Do we then make void the law through faith? GOD forbid. Yea we establish the law. The law is supremely excellent, the transcript of the Divine mind cannot be obeyed too much, but to CHRIST only must we look for everlasting salvation. We have no hope for time or for eternity which is not grounded upon the merits alone of that Saviour who offered Himself once for all, without money and without price, the guilty and the lost. But if we can say with our whole heart, " GOD forbid that I should glory save in the cross of our LORD JESUS CHRIST," then is He made of GOD unto us wisdom and righteousness, and sanctification and redemption—then are we the adopted members of His family, children of GOD through faith, and if children then heirs, heirs of GOD, and joint heirs with CHIRST—the Saviour has taken us by the hand, that He might lead us into green pastures, and by the still waters—the dark cloud of offended justice shall no more veil the heavens that hang over us, but the warm beams of the Sun of righteousness, the gladdening emanations which issue from the Most High shall flow copiously upon our souls, touching the springs of happiness and quickening the seeds of immortality within us. Thus shall we realize the enjoyment of a present salvation, and the dawning of a day everlasting. The night of sin and imperfection, of trial and obscurity, is already far spent, and the day is at hand. The bright beams of morning irradiate the tops of the distant hills, inviting us to gird up the loins of our minds, and to be sober, and hope unto the end for the grace that shall be brought unto us at the revelation of JESUS CHRIST. There, a glorious immortality is reserved for adopted sons. Long after it as your final and ultimate portion which sin has never sullied, which sorrow shall never corrode, and which your heavenly Father will give you as your inheritance forever. Anticipate it as your rest, peaceful and

refreshing after the labors of the day. Look
forward to it as your home, where in company
with GOD and CHRIST, and angels and all the
redeemed, you will dwell in perfect friendship
and go no more out.

CHAPTER III.

THE NATIVITY.

"When Christ was born in Bethlehem,
　'Twas night, but seemed the noon of day;
The stars whose light was pure and bright,
　Shone with unwavering ray."

The anniversary of the Nativity brings to us
thoughts of a precious Saviour; and angels and
men rejoice together in the glad history of His
love. This sacred festival of the Church is the
holiday season of the world, and pleasant memories are thus blended with joyous Christian feelings. Songs, and carols, and blazing hearths,
and happy greetings usher in the day, and cause

our life to be as merry as a marriage peal
Schools are dismissed, and stores are closed.
And amid houses bright with gifts, and churches
fresh with evergreen, devout affection breaks out
in songs of praise, " Hosannah, blessed be the
King of Israel that cometh in the name of the
LORD."

It matters not that some insinuate their doubts
whether the 25th of December be really the day
when CHRIST was born. It is the day which Christians, from a very early period, have chosen to
observe as such, and it answers every purpose
which any other day could answer in the celebra-
tion of this great event. It unites upon itself,
through a long observance, the hearts of the faith-
ful all over the world, and comes down to us
linked with such sunny memories of social gath-
erings and blessed services that it would be a
shock to the sensibilities of Christendom not to
improve the occasion for the glory of GOD, and
the good of the soul. Let any devout mind give
itself up on this day to meditating upon the incarnate Saviour, and we believe he will yield to
the impulse of falling on his knees with the burst
of grateful acknowledgment, " Thanks be unto

God for His unspeakable gift." So that if it could be shown that for eighteen centuries Christians have mistaken the day, and that we know not the precise time when the Son of God came down from the far heavens to this sin-stricken earth, still it would be unreasonable and absurd not to follow this goodly custom of the Church which has preserved for us the fact that "Unto us is born a Saviour which is Christ the Lord."

We hail the festival with cheerful hearts, greeting with smiles and wishes for happiness, the old and young. We decorate our temples with festoons, and stars, and Scriptural mottoes, in token of joy and gladness, and make them vocal with Te Deums in the sweet melody of song. Christmas speaks of Christ in loving accents. It declares that the great object for which He came into the world was to save sinners. The Church in her recognition of so fundamental a doctrine says that "God's blessed Son was manifested that He might destroy the works of the devil, and make us the sons of God, and heirs of eternal life." She also adds, that "God has given Him to be unto us a sacrifice for sin, and an ensample of godly life. These were the motives that prompted Him to undertake His earthward mission, and to live, labor, and die for a race of offenders. The inspired writers speak of His advent as a mystery. It is so referred to in our admirable Litany—" By the mystery of Thy holy incarnation—By thy holy nativity and circumcision." The children of faith must not pry into hidden secrets, but rejoice in the Advent, till the LORD shall lift the veil with His own hands, and exhibit the inscrutable mysteries of that wondrous affair as subjects of the clearest vision.

The birth of a person is always understood to signify his beginning or introduction into the land of life and among the living. It is the origin of a career of consciousness of which he had no existence anterior to the present. No matter what the doctrine of Pythagoras affirms about the pre-existence of spirit, and the transmigration of souls, no man could ever truthfully say that he had another life before this—no man, whether Chinaman or not, much as he may believe the absurdity, can presume to instruct us in the scenes and incidents that transpired in connection with other stages of His bein: in the depths of a dateless age. CHRIST only could speak of a life that He had spent elsewhere. The Son of the Eternal could say, "I came out from God"—"I came forth from the Father, and am come into the world"—"I leave the world, and go to the Father." "Before Abraham was *I am.* Your father Abraham rejoiced to see my day, and he saw it and was glad." Yea, so confidently did he speak of the blissful recollections of His pre-existent state that, lifting up His eyes to heaven, He said, "And now, O Father, glorify Thou me with Thine own self, with the glory which I had with Thee before the world was." These affirmations of divinity from His own lips are in beautiful harmony with the testimony of the New Testament writers. They were intimately acquainted with all the circumstances of His birth. They knew the predictions; and they believed His " goings forth were of old, from everlasting." They accordingly looked upon His assumption of our nature simply in the light of an arrival from another sphere—an advent—an incarnation—a mere incident in an existence that had no beginning. And while they surrendered to Him the supremacy of their affections, to which they conceived He was justly entitled, they congratulated the world on receiving so illustrious a visitor, and our humanity as enshrining so celestial an occupant. St. John in an allusion to His eternity says, " In the beginning was the Word, and the Word was with God, and the Word was God: and the Word was made flesh and dwelt among us." And the Apostle Paul tells us that " God, who, at sundry times, and in divers manners, spake in times past unto the fathers by the prophets, hath in these latter days spoken unto us by His Son: who, being in the form of God, thought it not robbery to be equal with God : but made Himself of no reputation, and took upon Him the form of a servant, and was made in the likeness of men—whose are the fathers, and of whom as concerning the flesh Christ came, who is over all, God blessed forever." Passages of this complexion have a peculiar charm thrown around them, proving as they do most conclusively that Christ was worshipped from eternity as God, before He "humbled Himself to be born of a virgin."

The birth of Jesus Christ formed the climax of a series of manifestations that have been vouchsafed under preceding economies. The first promise of the Saviour was given under the

identical tree where our first parents fell; and subsequent manifestations kept alive the expectation
of the event till it was fully realized.   When
Abraham was at Mamre, gray with the snows of
a hundred years, sitting on the threshold of his
Arab tent, and enjoying the fresh breeze astir, he
espied three men approaching him, two of them
were angels, and the third was the SON of GOD.
The Apostle commenting on the event, says, "Be
not forgetful to entertain strangers, for some have
thereby entertained angels unawares." The distinguished visitors partook of the patriarch's
friendly cheer, and resumed their journey.   Abraham accompanied them to an eminence from
which they obtained a view of the cities of Sodom
and Gomorrah.   And pointing to those silent
cities among the mountains as they lay embedded
in a paradise of luxuriant verdure, the Angel of
the Covenant informed him that this scene, so fair
and lovely, was doomed to become the theatre
of a most signal destruction on account of the
wickedness of the people.   The venerable patriarch, falling at the feet of the illustrious speaker,
earnestly interceded for the guilty inhabitants till
he hoped he had won a reprieve.   And that divine

personage with whom he pleaded was JESUS CHRIST, who afterwards enunciated the solemn truth, "No man hath seen GOD at any time; the only begotten SON who is in the bosom of the FATHER, He hath declared Him."

The leaves of time opened up another manifestation which occured one memorable night in the history of Jacob. Between him and Esau there existed a long-standing grudge about the birthright: and tidings had reached him that his offended brother was coming against him on the morrow with four hundred armed men. The patriarch, dejected and anxious, betook himself in his extremity to the GOD of Bethel, and felt in the ardor of his devotion a mysterious conflict as if a person were wrestling with him, "twisting, thrusting and straining, and striving to hurl him to the ground." The assault came from no enemy. His opponent was no other than the second person in the adorable Trinity; "the everlasting SON of the FATHER." "And Jacob called the name of the place Peniel—the face of GOD: for he said, I have seen GOD face to face, and my life is preserved." Thenceforth his name was no more called Jacob.

but Israel, because as a prince he had power with
GOD, and with man, and had prevailed.

The Israelites, in the process of events, became
bondmen in the land of Egypt, and the LORD revealed Himself to Moses at Horeb in a burning
bush. It was a most singular phenomenon, out-
shining in brightness the blaze of noon, and yet
occasioning no consumption of the leaves and
branches. These were reflected through the
excellent glory with beautiful transparency. And
when the astonished Hebrew turned aside to see
this great sight, it became vocal with instruction,
and said, "Draw not nigh—put off thy shoes from
thy feet: for the place whereon thou standest is
holy ground." And the voice went on to add,
"I am the GOD of thy Father—the GOD of Abraham—the GOD of Isaac, and the GOD of Jacob."
But for the assurance of the voice Moses might
have concluded that the whole exhibition was
simply the revelation of an angel: now he had
indisputable testimony that it was Jehovah JESUS,
who appeared to his progenitors—the same august
personage who afterwards conducted the exodus
by a pillar of cloud by day, and fire by night—the

same who supplied, miraculously, the migratory hosts with manna from the skies and water from the rock, and of whom it is said, " They did all eat the same spiritual meat; and did all drink the same spiritual drink: for they drank of that spiritual Rock that followed them; and that Rock was CHRIST"—the same whose voice shook the earth when the mountain of Sinai trembled to its base, and " now He hath promised—saying, yet once more I shake not the earth only, but also heaven : I will shake the heavens and the earth, and the sea, and the dry land; and I will shake all nations, and the desire of all nations shall come."

The LORD GOD, who thus bowed the heavens to talk with our ancient fathers, was indeed the long-promised, long-looked for Messiah. The glorious being with whom Enoch walked in the age of the antediluvians was the predicted Saviour with whom the disciples walked on the road to Emmaus. He who said to Moses, " Certainly I will be with thee," was the same sympathizing friend who said to the Apostles, " Lo I am with you always." The magnificent vision of the Divine glory, which Isaiah saw, exhibiting JEHOVAH as " high and lifted up," and whose " train filled the temple," while seraphs veiled their faces with their wings, and made the temple vibrate with their hymns of rapture, was a vision of the glory of CHRIST. The SON of man whom Nebuchadnezzar king of Babylon saw walking with the three Hebrew youths in the midst of the burning fiery furnace, was the same SON of man who came to seek and to save them that are lost. The Ancient of Days that appeared to Daniel was the infant of Days that was born in a stable at Bethlehem. The manifestations were made susceptible of different modifications to suit different ages, but we can recognize, all through, the self-same Revealer of the FATHER, the self-same prophet of the Church—the self-same Saviour of our race—who is " CHRIST the LORD."

The birth of JESUS CHRIST came through a succession of persons who formed a consecutive line of genealogical descent. .Before the flood the prediction of CHRIST's advent was general and indefinite. There was nothing to indicate either the time or the place. The only thing absolutely certain in the matter was the fulfilment of the promise that the Deliverer should come. But, as centuries rolled along, it seemed good to the

Divine Being to institute a series of limitations, and to make the promise more restricted and precise. Agreeably with this narrowing process the LORD fixed upon Abraham, of Ur of the Chaldees, and pronounced him the chosen progenitor of the Messiah. The first of an illustrious line, he was to be separated from all the rest of the world to serve GOD in sincerity and in truth. There were born to him two sons, and the blessing was to flow through Isaac the younger. The land of Canaan was also given into his possession as a cradle for the approaching nativity. Over the family and the country thus selected the care of a special providence was exercised with unremitting attention, anticipating every circumstance, and rendering the most untoward events subservient to incarnate Deity. The history of the twelve sons of Jacob, though unpromising for a time, was made to form a conspicuous part in the arrangement, as there was one of that number to whom was awarded the honor of being a link in the chain of the lineage of CHRIST. The dying patriarch predicted that in Judah's line should the Shiloh come. "The sceptre shall not depart from Judah, nor a law-giver from between his feet, until Shiloh come ; and unto Him shall the gathering of the people be." Ages passed on, and the wandering tribes found themselves crossing the Jordan to take possession of the land. They were like the waves of the sea for multitude, or, as Balaam expresses it, "like valleys spread forth; as gardens by the river's side; as the trees of lignaloes which the LORD hath planted, and as cedar trees beside the waters." The LORD who rode upon the heavens in their help was eminently among them, enabling them to triumph in every place, and causing squadrons of their enemies to melt before them like wax, till the chosen country literally swarmed with the chosen race.

During one of the subsequent generations the land of Israel was visited with a sore famine, and many of the people were induced to leave the place of their birth, to sojourn in foreign countries. Among others, Elimelech and his wife Naomi removed with their family to Moab. The inspired narrative informs us that " he went out full," but soon died, leaving a widow and two sons in a strange land. The sons took to themselves wives of the women of Moab, and settled in that country. This was an open violation of the express injunction of heaven not to marry with idolaters. But the LORD overruled it in this instance for good, and made it the means of bringing to the knowledge of the truth a Moabitess woman, and uniting her to the ancestry of David as an indispensable link in the genealogy of CHRIST. Only a few years elapsed before the two sons, Mahlon and Chilion, were cut off, and their wives became widows. Naomi now resolved to leave the land of her sorrows, and return to her pious kindred and acquaintance in Judea. Her daughters-in-law determined to accompany her at least a part of the journey. When they had proceeded some distance, the venerable woman, anxious to save them from fatigue, admonished them to return, each to her mother's home. The pious Ruth continued to cleave to her, adding, "Entreat me not to leave thee; for where thou goest I will go, and where thou lodgest I will lodge: thy people shall be my people, and thy GOD my GOD." With such gushings of affection it were cruel on the part of Naomi to say another word to dissuade her. They accordingly traveled on together, ruminating upon the events of the past, and conflicting with apprehensions of the

future—behind them the graves they loved, and
before them a dark uncertain. They arrived in
Bethlehem some time about the end of summer,
when the fields were waving with the various
products of the earth, and the golden grain, and
the tasseled corn, and the verdant grass bespoke
the wisdom and goodness of GOD, " Who causeth
grass to grow for the cattle, and herb for the service of man."   Here the character of Ruth shone
forth in truth and loveliness. Though accustomed
to rank and affluence, she entered the fields as a
gleaner, and trained her delicate hands to the
rough usage of a day-laborer.   Boaz, who was a
mighty man of wealth, and of the family of Elimelech, saw her with the gleaners; and on being
told the relation she sustained to Naomi, and her
attachment to the people of GOD, resolved to take
her as his wife: and thus the beautiful gleaner
of the fields of Bethlehem became the great-grand-
mother of the king of Israel; and the family of
Elimelech, which was on the border of extinction,
merged from gloom into splendor, and shone on-
ward through all the lineage of David, till it blended with the glory that appeared over the plains of
Bethlehem, when the chorus of angels was poured

on the midnight air, because the Saviour was cradled there in homeless solitude. If Ruth had acted as did Orpah, and returned to Moab, it is difficult to conceive how such sublime results could have been brought about. Upon the single point of her adherence to Naomi seemed to rest the comprehensive nature of the Christian Dispensation. The course she pursued can only be accounted for as the influence of principle; while He who sees the end from the beginning, determined to take this Gentile woman into the genealogical roll of the Saviour's pedigree, and give her the reward of her devotion in becoming the mother "of Obed, who was the father of Jesse, who was the father of David."

If the property of Boaz was kept secure, and handed down successively to the possession of each family respectively, then we have something like tangible proof that the fields on which Ruth was accustomed to glean were the same identical acres over which David led his father's sheep when he was a shepherd boy—the same fields over which he was casting his eye when he penned that beautiful Psalm, "When I consider thy heavens, the work of thy fingers," &c.—the same fields that furnished him with the smooth pebble stone when he went forth to meet Goliath, and the same fields where the shepherds were watching their flocks when CHRIST was born.

The promise was made to David about a thousand years before the Advent, that a son of his should possess universal empire. "He shall have dominion from sea to sea, and from the river unto the ends of the earth." "All kings shall fall down before him: all nations shall serve him. In his days shall the righteous flourish, and abundance of peace so long as the moon endureth." This did not apply to Solomon, though he was king in Jerusalem—his dominion vast—his reign pacific—his fame world-wide: and peace, and plenty, and the law's protection made gold like brass, and silver sheckels like stones of the street. There came a time when that Hebrew monarch gave his countenance to idolatry, and brought a blight over the Jewish commonwealth. The sun no longer smiled in Israel's sky. There was a dark discomfort in the air—the people murmured—the ways of Zion mourned—the kingdom became rent, and the twelve tribes of Israel were carried away into captivity. Yet wonderful was the wisdom

which prevented them from losing their national-
ity, and kept them a race distinct—wonderful the
providence which, while ten of the tribes were
lost, protected the family of Judah, and made sure
the captives' return to Zion with songs of rejoic-
ing—wonderful the goodness which brought in
the Saviour incarnate when the world was at its
greatest need, and the Romans had consolidated
the languages of the earth, and constructed their
arterial roads to transmit the tidings with the
wings of the wind—wonderful the faithfulness
which arranged that when the mission of CHRIST
was accomplished, the Jews should be punished
for their unbelief by their dispersion into all the
world, denying all their records, and "making
it utterly impossible that another Son of David
should be born in David's town."

The birth of JESUS CHRIST coincides beautifully
with ancient prediction as to time and locality.
The last blessing of Jacob to his sons contained
the prediction, that the coming Saviour should
not exceed the time during which the descendants of Judah should continue a united people,
and be governed by their own laws. The prophets Haggai and Malachi measured the time with

equal precision in reference to the temple. "Behold I will send my messenger, and he shall prepare the way before me: and the LORD whom ye seek shall suddenly come to His temple, even the messenger of the covenant, whom ye delight in: behold He shall come, saith the LORD of Hosts." "And the glory of this latter house shall be greater than that of the former." Need we clearer proof that the Saviour was to make His appearance in the second temple, and to grace and dignify it with His presence?—that He was to come during the continuance of the kingdom of Judah, and immediately subsequent to the prophet Malachi. The time as revealed to the prophet Daniel was just seventy weeks from the edict to rebuild the Holy City, after the Babylonian captivity. "Seventy weeks are determined upon thy people, and upon thy holy city." (Dan. ix. 24, 25, 26, 27.) Reckoning a day to mean a year would be four hundred and ninety years to the commencement of the Christian era. At the expiration of this period CHRIST came; the sceptre had departed from Judah, and the last remnant of the greatness of Israel was debased into a province of Syria. This was what St. Paul calls *the fulness of time*—

the Augustan age, and the best adapted for introducing the Saviour and His gospel. The world was at peace. The wars of long centuries had ceased. And the minds of men had leisure to listen to His teachings, and decide whether He was the true Messiah or not. Both Jews and Gentiles had political motives to urge them to this. The Jews were under the Roman yoke, and looked forward to the Messiah as their Deliverer. He was a bright star in their horizon; and they were prepared to scrutinize His character with the nicest accuracy. The heads of the Roman government were also jealous of losing any portion of their influence, and they would consequently investigate his credentials with the closest vigilance. The two parties had been ably disciplined for the task by the system of argumentation that had been introduced, and which admitted nothing without proof. Christianity, therefore, threw down the gauntlet, and challenged research. The collisions and disputes that ensued served to rub the diadem into brightness, and to manifest to the world that CHRIST was certainly He that should come, and that they need not look for another.

The delay of the Advent four thousand years was because there was no other epoch so favorable.   Only a few centuries before the nations of the earth were in such a state of internal antagonism, that the inhabitants of one country could not cross over the frontiers and sojourn, even for a short time, in another.   But owing to the conquests of Alexander, and afterwards of the Cæsars, the whole civilized world became consolidated into one empire, and an appeal to Cæsar was deemed a sufficient protection in almost every capital and village of the habitable globe.   It was therefore a time when Christianity would tell upon the world with the greatest possible emphasis.   Another important consideration was the prevalency of the Greek language.   This was now spoken by so many cultivated nations that a truth uttered in Greek would find an echo everywhere, while the same truth, if spoken in Hebrew, would scarcely be understood beyond the limits of Judea. Hence the wisdom of the arrangement which deferred the Incarnation till the enemies of the Gospel had prepared the means for embodying its truths in the most expressive and permanent shape, so that they might be proclaimed with the greatest ease; be understood by the greatest number, and reach the utmost limits of the human family.

It is no less remarkable that the same restrictive process which fixed on a particular nation, the nation of the Jews—a particular tribe, the tribe of Judah—a particular family, the family of David; and a particular virgin, the virgin Mary, should determine, also, that the little town of Bethlehem should be the predestined and distinguished locality. "And thou Bethlehem Ephrata, though thou be little among the thousands of Judah, yet out of thee shall He come forth unto me that shall be ruler in Israel." It was indeed little among the thousands of its neighbors, remarkable neither for the elegance of its buildings, nor the commerce of its people, nor the number of its inhabitants, but aggrandized by the promise of an event that should make it illustrious in the annals of eternity.

And now that the time has come to manifest the Godhead in human form, where are Joseph and Mary? Where is the reputed father of our LORD, and where the blessed among women? They are away off in yonder village of Nazareth, in the province of Galilee, dwelling together in rural seclusion, and waiting with expectation the event desired of all nations. They repair to the synagogue to hear the law and the prophets, and sing the songs of Zion; and the soul of Mary, encouraged by the announcement of the angel, rises to heaven in the tuneful inspiration of her own splendid Magnificat, "My soul doth magnify the LORD, and my spirit hath rejoiced in GOD my Saviour. For He hath regarded the low estate of His handmaiden; for behold, from henceforth all generations shall call me blessed. For He that is mighty hath done to me great things; and holy is His name." Marvelous, as if by the special decree of heaven, the Roman Emperor now determines to take a census of all the people in his dominions, and requires them to appear for enrollment at the head-quarters of their respective families. The lineal descendants of David must present themselves in David's city. Joseph and Mary must therefore undertake a journey to Bethlehem. The city was full. There was much buzz and excitement. They could obtain no accommodation, either at a public inn, or in a private lodging. And, weak and weary, they were glad to avail themselves of the humble retirement of a stable. And so it was that while they were there "the days were accomplished that she should be delivered. And she brought forth her first born son, and wrapped Him in swaddling clothes, and laid Him in a manger." That new born babe was CHRIST the LORD—that infant was the royal Saviour—that cradle contained heaven's greatest gift—earth's brightest benediction. There lay the Mighty GOD, the everlasting FATHER, the Prince of Peace—the Omnipotent Creator and upholder of all things—the Resurrection and the Life—the embodiment of all the attributes of Deity—the Light to lighten the Gentiles, and the glory of His people Israel. *There* was that majestic Being whom all heaven adore—whom all powers obey—whom every eye shall see—to whom every knee shall bow.

> Cold on His cradle the dew-drops are shining ;
> Low lies His head with the beasts of the stall ;
> Angels adore Him, in slumber reclining,
> Maker and Monarch, and Saviour of all."

Sweeter and softer strains never fell on the ears of humanity, than when angels in the splendor of that memorable night sang, "Glory to GOD in the highest, and on earth peace, good-will towards men." They cheer the spirit of the faint, and stir the hopes of the disconsolate, disposing us to pray, "Evermore sing us this song." The tune, so musical, was the earnest of a future and glorious harmony; the prelude to a grand and universal chorus. We must not suppose the anthem was meant to be construed simply in the light of a *prayer*, Glory *be* to GOD—Peace *be* on earth, and good-will *be* to men; but it affirms such to be already the case; not indeed fully and finally, but in principle and in the bud, limited and repressed at present, but gradually unfolding. There is more of GOD revealed in that angelic ascription, "Glory to GOD in the highest," than in the sky and the earth together. It is a passage so grand, that if the very stars were its syllables, and the concave of heaven its pages, they would be altogether inadequate to express the grandeur of its truth. Astronomy, Botany, Philosophy, Science and Literature ought not to be mentioned in the same breath with it. It tells us of mercy in the highest, truth in the highest, love in the highest, power in the highest; and all these scattered rays combine in one focus, Glory to GOD in the highest—Glory in the highest strains—in the highest heavens—by the highest angels, and by the highest number of saints.

The next note in the song announces peace on earth—peace to assuage the angry passions of men; to tranquilize their troubled spirits, and to induce a feeling of amity and concord that shall lead them to dwell together in love and unity. The olive branch of peace needs only to be waved over the nations of the earth, and the demon of war shall die; the temple of Janus shall be closed; the sword shall be put into its scabbard, and a voice louder than a thousand thunders shall be heard above the tumults of the world, Peace, be still. Only let CHRIST be universally recognized, loved and adored, and earth shall enjoy a peace such as it never had before; its holy current will rush through every channel; its pure waters shall allay every passion; its presence calm every storm. That cold avalanch which now lies heavy and chill upon the heart of shivering humanity shall be removed, and earth once more look beautiful and bright.

The most consoling note of all is, good-will to men—not good-will to the angels that sinned;

to the spirits that fell, but good-will to *men*—good-will to men in the hour of penitence and sorrow —good-will to men in the season of affliction— good-will to men in the solemn article of death— good-will to men in the solemn scenes of judgment—good-will to men through the ages of eternity.

But for this announcement of good will, the natural suspicion of our hearts would have led us to expect just the contrary. We should have feared that CHRIST was coming to call us to an account for our sins, and to vindicate His violated law. But "GOD sent not His SON into the world to condemn the world, but that the world through Him might be saved." The first appearance of the angel to the shepherds to announce His advent created consternation and alarm. They were sore afraid. And it was not till he had gained their confidence, and overcome their fears and apprehensions, that they listened with joy to the multitude of the heavenly host. The Shepherds now said, "Let us go even to Bethlehem, and see this thing which is come to pass, which the LORD hath made known to us." The Shepherds were probably among the number of persons who were

looking for redemption in Jerusalem. Perhaps
at that very moment they were silently musing
when the kingdom of GOD should come, sighing
in the language of David, " O that the salvation
of GOD were come out of Zion! When GOD
bringeth back the captivity of His people, Jacob
shall rejoice, and Israel shall be glad." They
delayed not to put their purpose into execution.
They went to Bethlehem, and told Joseph and
Mary what it was that brought them. They ex-
plained the angels' visit—caught a glimpse of the
new born king, and went home praising the LORD
for the abundance of His mercy. Never after
could they forget those plains. They would tread
them as hallowed ground. When they slept, it
would be in expectation of receiving some fresh
revelation. And starting up in the stillness of
night, they would listen to imaginary sounds,
fancying that an ærial orchestra was floating by.
Gaze on the amazing scene of Deity incarnate.
Ponder over the wondrous exhibition of Redeeming love. Fear not to believe in Jesus too soon,
nor to rejoice in Him too much. Let the love of
GOD your Saviour flow in a full tide upon your
cold and wintry souls. Open your hearts to re-

ceive Him, and it will make your feelings happy,
and your dispositions new.

CHAPTER IV.

THE SONG OF ANGELS.

THE sentiment of the Apostle, that the love of
CHRIST passeth knowledge, is a truth to which
every renewed mind will yield a cheerful assent.
It has heights which cannot be scaled—depths
which cannot be fathomed—breadths which cannot be measured, and lengths which cannot be
told.   The tenderest exhibition that we have
of it is in the work which He came to accomplish.   Visiting us in our low estate of degrada-
tion and misery, His mission is fraught with the
liveliest interest, whether considered in reference
to the GODHEAD, as unfolding the brightest display
of the Divine perfections, or as securing to the
millions of the human family the blessings which
are to be enjoyed through the ages of eternity.

It develops emotions of far deeper intensity than any that are comprised in the sacrifices that men are wont to make to secure the objects of their aspiration. Almost everywhere persons are to be met with who are willing to travel far for worldly gain, and to expose themselves to danger and death in the accumulation of wealth.

But JESUS came from the far heavens to this sin stained earth, and though "rich, yet for our sakes became poor, that we, through His poverty, might be made rich." Some travel far to obtain fame and distinction. The Saviour made Himself of no reputation, and took upon Him the form of a servant. Some visit distant countries for the improvement of their health, and the prolongation of their lives. CHRIST gave Himself up unto death, the death of the cross, that He might be a full, perfect and sufficient sacrifice for the sins of the world. The words, "Glory to GOD in the highest, and on earth peace, good-will toward men," embody the song that was sung by a choir of angels on the joyful occasion of His nativity. Sweeter and softer strains never fell on the ears of humanity. They cheer the spirits of the faint, and stir the hopes of the disconsolate, disposing

us to pray, Evermore sing us this song. It was
first heard in delightful echoes on the plains of
Bethlehem; and the tune then started was the
earnest of a future and glorious harmony—the
prelude to a grand and universal chorus. The
anthem was not meant to be construed simply in
the light of a prayer, Glory *be* to GOD—Peace *be*
on earth—Good-will *be* to men, but it affirms such
to be already the case. Not indeed fully and
finally, but in the principle and in the bud—limited and repressed at present, but gradually unfolding. And when the Sun of Righteousness
shall arise and shine in vertical splendor, the glory
shall be unshrouded, the peace unbroken, and the
still small voice of Bethlehem swell into the voice
of a great multitude, and as the voice of many
waters, and as the voice of many thunderings,
saying, "Alleluia, for the LORD GOD omnipotent
reigneth."

We recognize in this song of the angels the
consecutive and dependent notes; the brightness
of the Divine glory, and the excellency of Divine
influence.

I. *The first note in the song is the Brightness of the
Divine Glory.* It is recorded of the shepherds

who were keeping watch over the flocks by night, that the glory of the LORD shone around them. These shepherds were probably among the number of those who were looking for redemption in Jerusalem, and may have been conversing together at this particular juncture, when the Kingdom of GOD should come; sighing in the language of David, "O that the salvation of GOD were come out of Zion;" when lo, suddenly and unexpectedly, an angel appeared to announce the desired intelligence; and a multitude of the heavenly hosts expressed their joy in the chorus, "Glory to GOD in the highest."

The most absorbing thought in the minds of angels is GOD's glory. They look at everything in relation to this. The rescue of perishing sinners from everlasting death they conceive to be the noblest manifestation of glory, demanding glory in the highest strains, glory among the highest beings, glory in the highest heavens, and glory from the whole universe of GOD, in the highest possible manner. It is very probable that up to the time of CHRIST's birth the angels had only obscure intimations of the plan of redemption. The cherubim who bended over the ark seemed to denote by their attitude a desire to look into those things that GOD had not fully revealed to them of His great purpose of mercy.

St. Paul speaks of the manifold wisdom of GOD, now made known by the Church unto the powers and principalities in heavenly places, as something to which the highest created intelligences were strangers, till it was made known to them at the Incarnation. Then it was that the secret burst upon angels and archangels, that Deity had united itself to humanity, and those heavenly beings at once made the amazing discovery an occasion of loud ascription of praise.

The infinite and eternal JEHOVAH could not be expected, in a work of such astonishing magnitude, to propose anything short of His own glory as the ultimate and final result of His designs. And just in proportion as finite minds are conformed to His will, and impressed with a sense of His preëminence, they will be solicitous in all their actions, whether they eat or drink, or whatever they do, to do all to His glory. The glory of the creature is usually promoted by adding to him something which he does not possess; the glory of Deity by making known what He is. To give glory to God, therefore, is to adore Him for the manifestation of His love.

When Moses prayed, "I beseech Thee, show me Thy glory," he acknowledged the self-existent splendor of the Almighty, independently of His creatures, and craved a more enlarged development of the divine effulgence. He had already seen some visible manifestations of it at Horeb—at the Red Sea—in the falling manna—in the riven rock, and in the cloudy, fiery pillar; but he felt as though each disclosure only increased his desire for another. He therefore sought a yet further discovery. And God said to him, "I will make my goodness pass before thee;" and God passed by and proclaimed His Name, His glory and His goodness. These are all convertible terms that signify one and the same thing. They are so many separate rays that constitute the bright flame, too dazzling for mortal eyes to look upon otherwise than apart.

The glory of the Divine goodness is specially displayed in the work of redeeming love; goodness, whether we consider the objects of it to be sinners, rebels and enemies, or the means by which their deliverance from wrath is effected, and their restoration to happiness procured. We would certainly admire the goodness of a monarch, stooping from his throne of unbounded royalty and power, surrounded with all the insignia of despotic authority, covering continents with his armies, and oceans with his fleets, and surpassing in the grandeur of his achievements the most splendid exploits of ancient and modern times. We would laud and magnify him if he were to pass from the splendor of his court and the radiance of his royalty, with all the meltings of pity and compassion, to relieve a single family bowed down with wretchedness and despair. That single act would redound more to his glory than the most illustrious triumphs of his policy, or the most splendid success of his arms. Yet what a poor, paltry act of benevolence this, when compared with the love of God in giving us His Son. The Saviour had existed from all eternity in His own uncreated essence perfectly happy without us or our services. He had under His control a universe of worlds so vast, that if the whole system of which we form a part were at once to be annihilated, it would be no more felt than the subtraction of a blade of grass from the verdure of

the fields, or the fall of a leaf from the foliage of
the forest. Yet when man, who is but dust and
ashes, rebelled against His supreme majesty;
when he ventured to raise his puny arm against
One who could have crushed him, the compas-
sionate Saviour resolved to interpose for his rescue—resolved to visit this insignificant spot in
the realms of being; to assume the body of man,
that is a worm; to descend to the lowest recesses
of sorrow and woe; to die an ignominious death
upon the cross; to make an atonement for sin, and
reconciliation for iniquity, and to raise countless
multitudes to happiness sublimer than that of
Eden, and to honors more exalted than those of
the angels; to raise them, indeed, to the very
throne of Deity, the All and in All. Was ever love
so disinterested, stupendous, infinite? The FATHER
smiled at the Advent with inexpressible tenderness. The groans of creation were hushed into
a momentary stillness. Angels rested from their
customary employment, and presented themselves
as admiring spectators of the wonderful scene.
And man that was a rebel was pardoned—man
that was a wanderer was reclaimed—man that
was condemned was absolved, and man that was

accursed was redeemed. "Blessing and honor and glory and power, be unto Him that sitteth on the throne, and unto the Lamb forever." Conspicuous in this mighty transaction is the justice of the angelic ascription, "Glory be to God in the highest."

The attribute of Divine wisdom is most beautifully unfolded in the same wonderful economy. CHRIST is expressly called the wisdom of God; and the Gospel which He proclaimed the wisdom of God in a mystery. The Gospel is a revelation from Him. It reflects His likeness, and directs us to Him, in whom are all the treasures of wisdom and knowledge. Every page of it shines in His light. Every text is a diamond radiant with His brightness. We see wisdom in the constitution of CHRIST'S person, so that while as man He could suffer affliction and death—as God He could vanquish the destroyer, and become enthroned and glorified. We see wisdom in such an adjustment of the Divine perfections with the purposes of mercy, that we are healed by the Saviour's wounds, crowned by the Saviour's cross, enriched by the Saviour's poverty, and glorified by the Saviour's disgrace. We see wisdom in the arrangement that renders God's displeasure against sin more apparent in pardoning than in punishing it, and in humbling the sinner's pride by those very considerations that tend to inspire his confidence, so that while he confesses himself unworthy of the least of God's mercies, he is encouraged to claim a participation in the greatest of His favors. This privilege alone affords ample scope for the exclamation, "Glory to God in the highest."

Nor can we fail to discover, in this magnificent enterprise, a most wonderful development of the glory of the Divine power. We usually associate the power of God with the formation of the fabric of the universe, and the revolution of the planetary systems of which the universe is composed. But all the manifestations of Omnipotence in the works of creation and providence are like the moon-beams, when compared with that which is presented us in the mediation of Christ. What though His birth was humble; was there not power in the commotion that was everywhere visible, causing all the acts of free agents to be subservient to the great purpose of the Incarnation? What though His death was ignominious; was there not power exerted amid the agonies of

the crucifixion, in the reclamation of a blasphem-
ing malefactor, and the reception of his renovated
spirit to paradise as a trophy of grace? Was
there not power when He bore for us the burden
of that wrath, which would otherwise have sunk
us to the lowest and deepest abyss; when He abol-
ished death, and destroyed him that had the power of death, that is the devil, and delivered them
who through fear of death, were all their lifetime
subject to bondage? Was there not power in the
astonishing success that uniformly attended the
first preaching of the Gospel, and that caused the
banner of the cross to be elevated above the
palace of the Cæsars? And is there not power in
the emancipation from the thralldom of corruption
of the thousands of our race who are now conse-
crating all their faculties, and all the duration of
their being, to the utterance of the Redeemer's
praise? O, where is the individual who, if he give
the subject only a cursory consideration, is not
prepared, with overwhelming gratitude, to chime
in with the angelic ascription, " Glory to God in
the highest."

That one beautiful passage, " God so loved the
world that He gave His only begotten Son," re-

veals more of GOD's wisdom and power and love
than the earth and the sky together. It is so
grand, that if the very stars were its syllables,
and the concave of heaven its pages, they would
be altogether inadequate to express the grandeur
of its truth. It is so simple that a child can understand it; and so rich that eternity will not
exhaust its fulness. The arts and sciences ought
not to be spoken of in the same breath with it.
And there is something strangely wrong in any
heart that can hear such tidings enunciated without a responsive thrill of ecstacy and joy. The
theme summons your contemplation to an exhibition of mercy in the highest; truth in the highest;
justice in the highest; love in the highest; power
in the highest; and all these scattered rays combine in one focus of glory to GOD in the highest—
glory in the highest heavens, by the highest
angels, and by the highest number of saints.

II. *We will now turn to the excellency of Divine
influence.* "Peace on earth." This was never
more needed than in the present troubled state of
the nations. We are thankful for anything that
transpires in the course of our pilgrimage which
makes a momentary lull. Wars, and rumors of

wars, battles and battle-fields are the staple of history. The most hideous of the train of sin is this gigantic evil that afflicts our world. It has immolated, from first to last, more individuals than are now to be found on the surface of the globe. But for a restraining providence human society must long since have become extinct; the last man would have expired, and GOD would have been despoiled of the revenue of His praise. The peace, so essential to assuage the angry passions of men, is the peace of the Prince of Peace; the peace that is inspired by truth, and sustained by righteousness. This it is that tranquilizes the troubled spirit, transforms the lion into a lamb, and induces a feeling of amity and concord that leads brethren to dwell together in love and unity. One of the fundamental principles of the Gospel is, "Thou shalt love thy neighbor as thyself." And its great, unalterable maxim is, "If thine enemy hunger, feed him; if he thirst, give him drink, for in so doing thou shalt heap coals of fire on his head." Only let the spirit of this Scriptural rule be generally exemplified; let men act it out in deference to Divine authority, and the demon of war shall die; the temple of Janus shall be closed, the sword shall be put into its scabbard, the olive branch of peace shall be waved over the earth, and a voice, in soothing undertones, shall be heard, subduing the tumults of the world, "Peace, be still." We know of nothing more alien from the pacific principles of the Gospel than storm and tempest. The Christ-loving disciple in whom the spirit of the Master breathes, yearns for a quiet element as the earnest of his coming rest. And so far as the blessed message of pardon from the skies is fully received and enjoyed, war with GOD and man will end, and peace will reign, such as earth saw never. Its holy current will rush through every channel, its pure waters allay every passion, its presence calm every storm, and the turbulent elements of our race repose in the calm serenity of a summer's eve. That cold avalanch which now lies heavy and chill upon the heart of shivering humanity needs only to be removed, and the fallen world will once more look beautiful and bright. Glory will shine resplendent on every mountain-top, sparkle in every rolling star, sound in the loud thunder, and murmur in the melodies of the passing breeze. All creation will resemble one grand oratorio, causing the key-note that sounded in the chimes of Bethlehem to swell into one glorious anthem of adoration and praise. In thought and word, in affection and action, the peace of GOD shall pulsate, which passeth all understanding.

Need we wonder that the peace legacy which CHRIST left with His disciples, when He said, "Peace I leave with you," is the subject of one of the most prominent invocations in our Church service? There is a Collect for morning and evening, very appropriately entitled a Collect for Peace; and it is much more comprehensive of meaning than the majority of worshipers have any idea of. There is a rich treasure underlying the prayer for outward peace from worldly enemies, that has specific reference to that inward peace, which leads to life eternal. Try and follow me in your reflections one moment, while I quote the one for Morning Prayer to be used immediately after the Collect for the day. "O GOD, who art the Author of peace, and lover of concord; in knowledge of whom standeth our eternal life; Whose service is perfect freedom; Defend us, thy humble servants, in all assaults of our enemies, that we, surely trusting in thy defence, may not fear the power of any adversaries, through the might of JESUS CHRIST our LORD." The humble Christian, lifting his heart to GOD in this formula, prays with the spirit, and with the understanding; and the Author of peace and lover of concord so fills him with joy and peace in believing, that his peace flows as a river, and his righteousness as the waves of the sea.

The Peace Collect for the Evening is, if possible, still more explicit. It appeals to GOD as the source of all holy desires, good counsels and just works, and then asks that He would give unto His servants that peace which the world cannot give; that our hearts may be set to obey His commandments; and also, that by Him, we, being defended from the fear of our enemies, may pass our time in rest and quietness, through the merits of JESUS CHRIST our Saviour. It can never be admitted that a Christian man can heartily offer such invocations to his Father in heaven, and then court the tempest and the hurricane. The grace of GOD, exercising a hallowed influence upon his heart, makes him a son of peace; disposes him to seek peace; to follow after the things which make for peace; to live in peace; to stay

his mind on GOD, and enjoy perfect peace. The
sublime sweetness of this mental composure is
called by the Apostle of the Gentiles, " The peace
which passeth all understanding." It is a calm
in the midst of a storm. Were you standing on
the sea-shore, and saw a gale on the ocean, the
winds blowing a hurricane, the lightnings flashing,
the thunders roaring, and the billows of the deep
lashed into a foaming fury, forming caverns in
appearance, and graves in reality; were you to
witness these effects you would be at no loss to
account for the phenomena. You would natural-
ly attribute the troubling of the waters to the
violence of the wind. But if, in the midst of all
this war and rage of the elements, the ocean
should suddenly show a peaceful bosom, perfectly
smooth and glassy, not a ripple to be seen, it
would exhibit a peace which passeth understanding; a stillness which you could not explain.
And it would, in this respect, afford a beautiful
emblem of the peace of the Christian; a calm
within, while all is tumult and storm without.
As a most happy illustration from the pen of inspiration, turn to that beautiful passage which
closes the thirty-second chapter of the prophecies

of Isaiah, from the seventeenth verse. " My people shall dwell in a peaceable habitation, and in
sure dwellings, and in quiet resting places, when
it shall hail, coming down on the forest, and the
city shall be low in a low place."

The most consoling note in the angelic song is
Good-will to men. Not good-will to the angel
that sinned, to the spirits that fell, but good-will
to men; to men who are invited and elevated
to their vacant thrones. The Mediator, by obey-
ing and dying in our stead, removed those sepa-
rating causes which kept us far off from our Maker. He did not indeed render us the objects of
good-will, but made it honorable on the part of
GOD to show us good-will consistent with His attributes, to deal with us as no longer enemies. It
might, therefore, be accurately said when CHRIST
was born, there was good-will toward men. The
birth was the earnest of the world's redemption.
It was virtually the same thing. GOD and man
were now at peace; and those who sometime
were afar off were made nigh by the blood of
CHRIST.

The announcement of good-will to men is without limitation. It is not an offer made to some,

and kept back from others. It appeals to all, without exception or reserve. It recognizes no outcast, but makes one comprehensive sweep, including the whole of our species; all the individuals of all the families. There is no straitening with GOD—it all lies in the dark, cold and narrow suspicions that fill our own bosoms. The offer of good-will through CHRIST is to all and upon all them that believe. We wish to lodge this offer in your hearts. We wish to woo you into confidence. We wish to whisper peace and reconciliation to your souls. We wish to assure you, by the most convincing testimony, that all who will may come and drink of the water of life freely. As the Apostle Peter said to the assembled multitude on the day of Pentecost, Repent every one of you, so we are commissioned to say, Believe every one of you. Believe that CHRIST came not to destroy men's lives, but to save them. Believe that CHRIST wishes to be gracious. Believe that a door is opened in heaven, and that you may find a blessed home in the bosom of your FATHER. Try and catch the tune of the angelic ascription, and you will sing it in the ways of the LORD, in all its sweetness. Ponder upon those passages of

Scripture that have a direct and immediate reference to the wonderful exhibition of Redeeming love. Ponder upon the words, " GOD commendeth His love toward us in that while we were yet sinners CHRIST died for us." Ponder upon the declaration, " GOD, Who is rich in mercy, for the great love wherewith He loved us, even when we were dead in sins, hath quickened us together with CHRIST, and hath raised us up together, and made us sit together in heavenly places in CHRIST JESUS." Ponder upon the text, " Not by works of righteousness which we have done, but according to His mercy, He saves us, by the washing of regeneration, and the renewing of the HOLY GHOST." Think of the good-will of GOD to your souls, continued under all your infidelity and rebellion, and antipathy and resistance with which you spurned the proffers of His mercy before you became members of His family; and the waywardness and indifference that you have manifested since you professed to love Him. Think of the good-will of GOD to your infirmities and wants, and say, O LORD, I will praise thee, for though thou wast angry with me, thine anger is turned away, and thou comfortest me. Think

of the good-will of GOD in the season of penitence
and sorrow and affliction; and let your light
afflictions, which are but for a moment, work out
for you a far more exceeding and eternal weight
of glory.   Think of the good-will of GOD in the
solemn article of death, and confront the last
enemy with the Resurrection song, " O Death,
where is thy sting?   O Grave, where is thy vic-
tory?"   Think of the good-will of GOD in the
solemn scenes of judgment, and anticipate the
approving welcome, " Well done good and faith-
ful servant, enter thou into the joy of thy LORD."
Think of the good-will of GOD to His people
through a ceaseless eternity, and say, " To Him
be glory and dominion for ever and ever."

Thus you see, if we advert only to the surface
of the subject, we are furnished with abundant
reason why the Song of Angels should be our song
to-day.   Let the tongue that has till now been
silent, chime in with the anthem of the heavenly
hosts, and praise its Maker in the highest strains.
Let the knee that has never been bent in prayer
before, bend now.   Let the obdurate and callous
heart dissolve in penitence and love.   Let the

solemn thought dwell on the mind, The friend or the foe of CHRIST.—which am I?

CHAPTER V.

CHRISTMAS DAY.

To CHRIST gave all the prophets witness: Isaiah predicted His nativity with a comprehensive outline of the glorious character that He should sustain, both in His humanity and divinity: "Unto us a child is born—unto us a son is given: the government shall be upon His shoulders, and His name shall be called Wonderful, Counselor, the Mighty GOD, the everlasting FATHER, the Prince of Peace." The blessing had not been actually given when this prophecy was delivered—only expected—yet it is proclaimed as a real history, and the subject of present enjoyment. The holy seer, as he wrote it, was so rapturously exultant in the blessedness of the event, that purpose and execution, promise and accomplishment, seemed the same thing. With GOD there is nothing future—nothing past. His being is one continued now—I AM, is His name, and this is His memorial in all generations. He calleth things that be not as though they were, saying, my counsel shall stand, and I will do all my pleasure.

Through a long series of ages the pen of prophecy had pointed to the birth of JESUS with remarkable distinctness. It foretold that He should descend from a particular nation—the nation of the Jews; from a particular Tribe—the Tribe of Judah; from a particular family—the family of David; from a particular virgin—the virgin Mary. He was also to come forth out of Bethlehem; and in that small but favored town He made His appearance. "And thou Bethlehem Ephratah, though thou be little among the thousands of Judah, yet out of thee shall He come forth that is to be ruler in Israel, whose goings forth have been of old, from everlasting." It was indeed small among the thousands of its neighbors—remarkable neither for elegance, nor commerce, nor the number of its inhabitants; but aggrandized, in the arrangements of Heaven, by an event which drew toward it a multitude of the heavenly host, who sang, "Glory to GOD in the Highest, and on earth, peace, good-will toward men."

Shepherds that night were in the fields watching their flocks. The glory of the LORD encompassed them. An embassy from the heavenly world communicated the blissful intelligence: "Unto you is born this day, in the city of David, a Saviour which is CHRIST the LORD." The shepherds hastened to the spot, and found the babe lying in a manger. The manger-cradled child was the child of promise, now clothed in the habiliments of humanity—the child of prophecy, who had verified the predictions of His birth in the minutest particular—the child of obscurity and poverty—the child of persecution and reproach—the child of renown—the child of the Highest. There prevailed at that time in the East a general expectation of the birth of some very extraordinary character. Balaam had announced the Messiah under the image of a star. "There shall come a star out of Jacob, and a sceptre shall arise out of Israel, and shall smite the corners of Moab, and destroy all the children of Sheth." When an unaccustomed star crossed

their field of vision, it arrested the notice of wise
men who came from the East to Jerusalem, saying, " Where is He that is born king of the Jews?
for we have seen His star in the East, and are
come to worship Him." They appeared to understand the connection between the sign and the
circumstance, or how could they have inferred
from the celestial phenomenon that the king of
the Jews was born? The star was altogether
supernatural; and it is not improbable that while
it engaged their attention, the Spirit of GOD impressed their hearts with a conviction of the relation and design. These wise men were probably
from Arabia or Chaldea, east of the Jordan.
They were devout men—serious and reflecting
men—men of a contemplative turn of mind, who
had renounced idolatry, and devoted themselves
to the worship of the Supreme Being. The object
of their visit was to attest the birth of the illustrious personage, and do Him homage. And if
they opened their treasures, and presented unto
Him gifts, gold and frankincense, and myrrh, it
was not more their grateful adoration, than the
fulfilment of what David and the prophet Isaiah
had declared, " The kings of Tarshish and of the

isles shall bring presents : the kings of Sheba and Seba shall offer gifts. They shall bring gold and incense, and they shall show forth the praises of the LORD. "The Gentiles shall come to Thy light, and kings to the brightness of Thy rising."

The people to whom He was immediately sent, were the lost sheep of the house of Israel. He came, a light to lighten the Gentiles, and the glory of His people Israel. He took not on Him the nature of angels, but the seed of Abraham. Good angels did not need His mediation, and bad ones were not permitted to share it. He became man that He might redeem man—one of us that He might rescue us from the ruins of the fall.

The several gradations of human condition were open to His acceptance, and of these He chose the lowest. The varieties of earthly splendor were in His estimation only as so many degrees of littleness and insignificance. If He had come in the pomp of state, the multitude would have been debarred from His presence, and the minds of men divided between the attractions of earthly rank, and the claims of celestial truth ; but by assuming the low condition of the majority, He made Himself accessible to all, and put forth truth

alone as the only object demanding their notice.
When He came down from heaven, He came not
to a throne, nor to a court, nor to ease and elegance, but to the cot of a poor carpenter. When
He might have spoken to His FATHER, and had
beside Him, in a moment, more than twelve le-
gions of angels, He chose for His companions
twelve poor fishermen. And when He hungered,
instead of calling to His aid the stores of heaven,
He partook, with His disciples, of their homely
fare—"They gave Him a piece of a broiled fish,
and of a honey-comb." What a lesson does this
teach us of the condescension of the SON of GOD!
What but love, pure, perfect and disinterested,
could brook such a painful ordeal? What stronger
evidence need we that He was born for us, and
for our salvation. The reduplication which occurs
in the prediction, "Unto us a child is born—unto
us a son is given," would seem to express the joint
action of the FATHER and the SON: that while
GOD so loved the world as to give His only begotten SON, the SON so loved us as to give Himself.
Whichever way we take of it, it was compassion
like a GOD. It comprised all gifts in one, and
was so liberal as to preclude the possibility of its

being ever said that GOD could give us more. "Beloved, if GOD so loved us, we ought also to love one another." The rugged paths we tread would then be smoothed; sunshine would fall on shady places; and calm and quiet would be the flow of life. "GOD is love; and He that dwelleth in love dwelleth in GOD, and GOD in Him." Of the Empire of the SON of GOD Isaiah affirms, "the government shall be upon His shoulders." The ancients had a custom of representing Atlas with the world on his shoulder. The world, with its mighty apparatus, does actually rest for its support on the Man CHRIST JESUS. "He supports all thing⁊ by the word of His power." "He is LORD of all." LORD of all might, majesty and dominion—LORD of all worlds—LORD of all creation—LORD of angels and archangels, and creatures animate and inanimate. "The LORD is king forever." His dominion is an everlasting dominion, and His kingdom is from generation to generation. From age to age, and from sphere to sphere, His government moves on, "none can stay His hand, or say, what doest Thou?" Looking down from the height of His holiness, He surveys, at a glance, the manifold movements of

His creatures, and with one single volition, can aid or thwart their schemes as may seem to Him good. "It is He that determines concerning a nation, and concerning a people, to establish or to destroy; to enlarge or to diminish." If the heathen rage, and the people imagine a vain thing; if the kings of the earth set themselves, and the rulers of the earth take counsel together against the LORD, and against His annointed, say- ing, "let us break their bands asunder, and cast away their cords from us, He that sitteth in the heavens shall laugh at them; the LORD shall have them in derision. He will speak unto them in His wrath, and vex them in His sore displeasuer." The reign of CHRIST is our solace in every vicissi- tude. No matter if clouds and darkness are round about Him, "righteousness and judgment are the habitation of His seat."

> " Blessings abound where'er He reigns,
>   The prisoner leaps to burst his chains;
>   The weary find eternal rest,
>   And all the sons of want are blessed."

This world is but a small fraction of His em- pire. The whole planetary system to which we belong is but a partial province of His government. There are other worlds, and other systems, the extent of which no measurement can calculate, and the number of which no arithmetic can compute, that are controled by the mysterious sway of the "Child born, the SON given." All are obedient to His behest, and are in His hands, as clay in the hands of the potter.

The names of CHRIST are expressive and appropriate. His Name shall be called Wonderful, Counselor, the mighty GOD, the everlasting FATHER, the Prince of Peace. This glowing constellation of names is illustrative of the infinite superiority of His person and character over every other.

Wonderful was CHRIST in His Incarnation: "The Word was made flesh, and dwelt among us." Wonderful in His humanity and divinity, combining in one person the finite and infinite—wonderful in His grandeur and humility—wonderful in His innocency and suffering—wonderful in His tenderness and severity—wonderful in His weakness and efficiency—wonderful in the blessings which He flung around Him. Wherever He went, disease and misery fled from His presence. Wherever He was expected the public way was

thronged with the helpless and the dying. Where
He had passed, life, health and happiness distinguished the path. The restored might be seen
making trial of their new found powers. Jesu's
voice was the first sound which many persons
heard—His form the first sight which many beheld
His name—the first word that many pronounced.
The victims of sorrow everywhere besought Him,
and never sought in vain. If the spiritual object of
His mission had permitted the continuance of His
abode on earth, He would have become the shrine
at which all disease would have knelt, and the
centre to which all suffering would have tended.
The world of the afflicted would have gone to
Him on a pilgrimage, and He would have healed
them all. He is "glorious in holiness, fearful in
praises, doing wonders."

The holy JESUS is Counselor, who gives counsel
to men. He was Counselor with the FATHER in
the work of creation; and when all things were
made by Him, and without Him was not anything
made—Counselor with the FATHER, in the work
of redemption, when in the divine and gracious
counsels, He became the "Lamb slain from the
foundation of the world"—Counselor with the

FATHER in the work of our sanctification, so that when "He ascended up on high, He led captivity captive, and received gifts for men, that the LORD GOD might dwell among them." The only wise GOD, our Saviour, in Him dwelleth all the fulness of the GODHEAD bodily. With Him are all the treasures of wisdom and knowledge. "Counsel is mine," says He, "and sound wisdom, I have understanding—I Wisdom dwell with prudence and find out knowledge of witty inventions." "The wisdom that cometh from above is pure and peaceable, gentle and easy to be entreated, full of mercy and good fruits, without partiality and without, hypocrisy." The light of the knowledge of the glory of GOD shines resplendently in CHRIST. He is "the image of the invisible GOD, the brightness of the FATHER'S glory, and the express image of His person."

CHRIST is the Mighty GOD —the Underived, Essential, Infinite, Almighty, King of kings and LORD of Lords. Mighty to accomplish His designs—mighty to perform His counsel—mighty to redeem—mighty to save—mighty to save unto the uttermost—mighty to reclaim—no case too desperate—nothing too hard. Far as we have wandered from His counsels, there is yet hope concerning us if we are disposed to return—Deeply as we have plunged into the vortex of crime and ungodliness, the mighty GOD is able and willing to restore us—Exiles and outcasts as we have been, the arms of the loving JESUS are outstretched to clasp us to His bosom and to His heart.

> "Mighty GOD, while angels bless Thee,
>   May we learn to lisp Thy Name;
> LORD of men as well as angels,
>   Thou art every creature's theme."

Do we revere the parental character? CHRIST is the Everlasting FATHER, or, as the Septuagint renders it, the FATHER of the everlasting age, or world to come. This is one of the most endearing relations under which we can think of Him. He has all the feeling, the affection and tenderness of a father durable in His nature. His love is everlasting attachment; His tenderness everlasting sympathy; His power everlasting protection. The saints of olden time could look up to Him, and say, "Doubtless Thou art our Father, though Abraham be ignorant of us, and Israel acknowledge us not: Thou, O LORD, art our Father, our Redeemer, Thy Name is from everlasting." "When my father, and my mother, forsake me," said David, "then the LORD will take me up." We look upon our earthly fathers and are reminded that, fondly as we may cling to them, they will die and leave us. The LORD's offspring can never be orphans. He lives forevermore; and because He lives we shall live also. With a fatherly feeling, He appeals to the sensibilities of our hearts, and calls us His children "I will receive you," says He, "and will be a FATHER unto you, and ye shall be my sons and daughters." The Saviour is celebrated as the FATHER of the fatherless, in that splendid song of triumph which St. Paul quotes in reference to the ascension. Hence, the LORD's Prayer may be addressed to CHRIST, in all its parts. We can scarcely imagine that, when in answer to the request of His disciples to teach them to pray, He composed and gave them a form, which should not include Himself as the object of their worship. It is a filial address of children to their Father, imploring the bestowment of blessings alike dear to Himself and to them.

JESUS is the PRINCE OF PEACE. CHRIST procures peace; reveals peace; imparts peace. Peace of

conscience; peace of mind; peace that passeth understanding. "Great peace have all they who love
His law." Peace is the legacy He bequeathed to
us. "Peace I leave with you, My peace I give
unto you." "The LORD blesseth His people out of
Zion, and causeth them to see the good of Jerusalem, and peace upon Israel," and when the nations
of the earth shall bow to Him, they shall learn war
no more. Glory to GOD on high—on earth be peace.

> " Like circles widening round,
>   Upon a clear blue river ;
> Orb after orb, the wondrous sound,
>   Is echoed on forever."

The theme of the Advent is one of overflowing
consolation, and exquisite tenderness—wonder-
fully realized in the issues of that night of nights,
which ushered in that memorable morn. Receive
in penitential faith, the loving Saviour to your loving hearts, and this will be to you a Christmas-
Day—a feast of the true Nativity—" CHRIST in
you the hope of glory.

www.ingramcontent.com/pod-product-compliance
Lightning Source LLC
Chambersburg PA
CBHW031929060726
47496CB00008BA/2612